Climbing
Kansas
Mountains

Climbing
Kansas
Mountains

BY GEORGE SHANNON

ILLUSTRATED BY THOMAS B. ALLEN

BRADBURY PRESS · NEW YORK

Maxwell Macmillan Canada Toronto
Maxwell Macmillan International
New York Oxford Singapore Sydney

The Kansas State bird is the western meadow lark;
the State flower is the sunflower.

Bradbury Press
Macmillan Publishing Company
866 Third Avenue
New York, NY 10022

Maxwell Macmillan Canada, Inc.
1200 Eglinton Avenue East
Suite 200
Don Mills, Ontario M3C 3N1

Macmillan Publishing Company is part of the
Maxwell Communication Group of Companies.

First edition
Printed and bound in the United States of America
10 9 8 7 6 5 4 3 2 1
The artwork was prepared with charcoal, pastel,
and colored pencils.
The text of this book is set in Aster.
Typography by Julie Quan

LIBRARY OF CONGRESS CATALOGING-IN-PUBLICATION DATA
Shannon, George.
Climbing Kansas mountains / by George Shannon ; illustrations by
Thomas B. Allen. — 1st ed.
p.   cm.
Summary: A young boy and his father share the magic of climbing
the "Kansas mountains."
ISBN 0-02-782181-1
[1. Kansas—Fiction.   2. Fathers and sons—Fiction.]   I. Allen,
Thomas B. (Thomas Burt), date. ill.   II. Title.
PZ7.S5287Cl   1993
[E]—dc20   89-38197

To my father, David Shannon,
who took me climbing,
and to Isamu Noguchi,
who helped me learn to see
—G. S.

To my friends,
the young readers
of Kansas
—T. B. A.

Once in the summer on a Sunday afternoon when there was nothing to do but wish for a quarter for the swimming pool, my father said, "Sam, time you and I went to climb a Kansas mountain."

"Sure," I said, "and watch pigs fly," like *he* always did when nothing made sense. He knew Kansas didn't have any mountains. He'd helped me make my flour-dough map that barely had a bump.

"Maybe, maybe not," he said as he gave my mom a wink. "It's up to you."

Either way it was better than staying at home, so I ran outside and hopped in the car. Just me—no brothers—in the big front seat.

When I asked, Didn't he remember how my map was flat, my father just smiled and said, "You'll see."

But all *I* saw was
the same old thing.
House after house
and the tiny park.
Uncle Roy's café
and the grocery store.

We passed the school
with its broken slide.
Then the old yellow house
where I learned to walk.

All the way through town
on one straight street,
everything in the distance
always wrinkled from the heat.

Block after block,
then over the tracks
at the edge of town
to the grain elevators
where my father worked,
moving shovel after shovel
of wheat all day.

When my father
stopped the car
and began to grin
his "got you" grin,
I suddenly knew
and began to grin, too.
"*These* are the mountains
you were talking about?
Elevator mountains
filled with wheat?"

"Why not?" he asked back. "The thing that makes a mountain is a high, quiet view. Are you ready?"

"Ready!"

Inside, as we climbed, my father told me of the times he'd climbed before—like the day I was born—step, step over step—up as high as eight houses stacked like blocks.

When we got to the top we didn't say a word. We could talk anywhere but couldn't see all this anyplace but here.

Everyone I knew,
every garden, every house
was *way* down below,
with cool wide sky
between there and me.

The school would have fit
in my desk *at* school, and
our house was hiding
under trees like a sneaky cat.

Fields of wheat still gold
and others cut to brown were all
as small as our own little
square of beans at home.

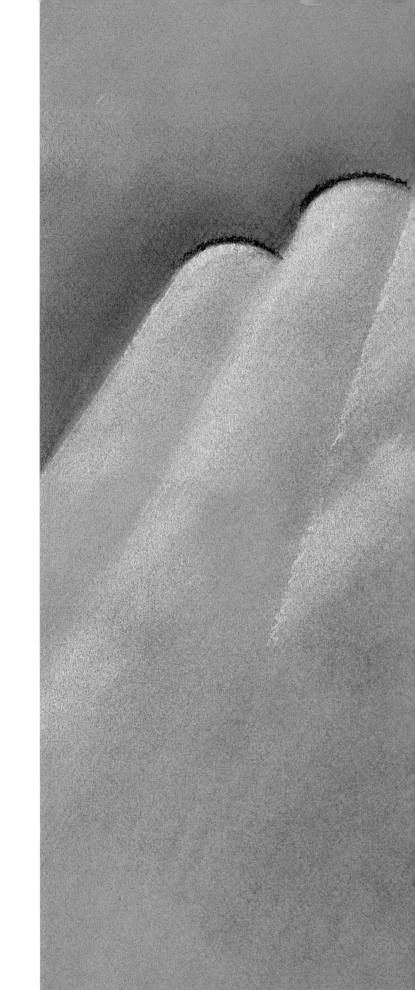

There were squares as smooth as fancy pants and squares plowed up like corduroy. Squares of squares and swirls and stripes. All held together like our tablecloth, but with ribbons of road instead of red.

All flat like the table in the dining room. A table grown so big it has no edge. A table so big the trees in town are its green centerpiece. A table so big it has a mountain of wheat for a giant to eat. A table so big…

"Ready?" said my father.
"Nearly suppertime."

"Ready," I said,
trying not to grin,
"to drive across the table
and through the centerpiece."

"Do what?" he said.
Then, "Got me!"
as he grinned a giant grin.
"Let's drive across the table
to the table at home."

Ever since then, when my father says, "How's about a drive across the table to the mountains and back?" *I'm* the only one who knows what he really means. Sharing time together. Just me—no brothers—in the big front seat.

About the Author

GEORGE SHANNON remembers his early years in Kansas vividly and says, "The town I grew up in is very much like the one Tom Allen has drawn." Known for his storytelling and such books as *Oh, I Love!* and *Dancing the Breeze*, both published by Bradbury Press, George Shannon now lives in Eau Claire, Wisconsin.

About the Artist

THOMAS B. ALLEN is the celebrated illustrator of such books as *Going West* by Jean Van Leeuween, recently starred by *School Library Journal*, and *In Coal Country* by Judith Hendershot, a *New York Times* Best Illustrated Children's Book and a *Boston Globe/Horn Book* Honor Book for Illustration.

He recalls his childhood days amidst the rolling hills of middle Tennessee in his own story, *On Grandaddy's Farm*.

Thomas B. Allen now lives in Lawrence, Kansas, where he is currently Hallmark Distinguished Professor in the Department of Design at the University of Kansas.